Magnificent Tales

Food for a Fish

The Whopping Story of Jonah and the Whale

Based on Jonah 1–3

Kelly Pulley

David C Cook

transforming lives together

FOOD FOR A FISH
Published by David C Cook
4050 Lee Vance View
Colorado Springs, CO 80918 U.S.A.

David C Cook Distribution Canada
55 Woodslee Avenue, Paris, Ontario, Canada N3L 3E5

David C Cook U.K., Kingsway Communications
Eastbourne, East Sussex BN23 6NT, England

LCCN 2012940692
ISBN 978-1-4347-0366-8
eISBN 978-1-4347-0510-5

Art and Text © 2012 Kelly Pulley

The Team: Susan Tjaden, Amy Konyndyk, Jack Campbell, Karen Athen

Manufactured in Hong Kong, in July 2012 by Printplus Limited.
First Edition 2012

1 2 3 4 5 6 7 8 9 10

071712

God loves *all* of His people.
He loves them a lot.
The ones who do good
and the ones who do not.

The people of Nineveh
weren't doing good.
The things that they did
weren't the things that they should.

So God said to Jonah, "Please do what I say.
Go to Nineveh now! Leave at once! Don't delay!
Tell the people I love them and not to do bad,
or they will be punished, and I will be sad."

Jonah thought to himself,
"A trip there won't be fun.
I will go somewhere else, like a beach in the sun.
The Nineveh people are grumpy and rude,
like they woke from a nap in a terrible mood."

Jonah liked his new thinking.
He liked it a lot.
"I'll hide out in Tarshish!
I know just the spot!"

"I'll do what I want!
Do what I want to do!
All I need to escape
is a boat and a crew!"

So he sneaked on a boat,
which he thought was quite smart.
But God wasn't fooled,
for He *knew* Jonah's heart.

Then God made a storm,
and the rain began lashing!
The wind was whish-whooshing!
The waves were splish-splashing!

The boat started tilting and tossing about!
The sailors hung on so they wouldn't fall out!

All the sailors cried out,
"We must do something quick,
or this splishing and splashing
will make us seasick!"

So they ran to wake Jonah,
who slept down below.
"Tell us *what* we should do!
Tell us *now* so we'll know!"

"I've been running from God.
Now He's angry with me.
Throw me out of the boat.
Throw me into the sea."

So they did what he said,
and the rain stopped its lashing.
The wind stopped whish-whooshing.
The waves stopped splish-splashing.

All the sailors were happy,
but Jonah was not.
He was under the sea.
He was in a bad spot!

But God rescued Jonah
and granted his wish!
God spared him from drowning ...
inside a big fish!

Three days and three nights
he spent inside its belly.
It was damp,
it was dark,
and oh boy
was it smelly!

Jonah knew he'd been wrong
to try running away.
So he looked in his heart
for the words he should say.
Then he lowered his head
and got down on his knees.
And he prayed prayers to God,
pleading, "God, hear me please.
You saved me from drowning
here inside this fish.
I'll do what You want,
do whatever You wish."

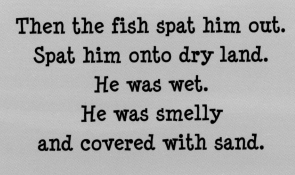

Then the fish spat him out.
Spat him onto dry land.
He was wet.
He was smelly
and covered with sand.

Jonah shook off the sand
with a brush and a flick.
Started walking to town,
started walking quite quick.

To the people he shouted
as loud as he could,
"Stop doing what's bad
and start doing what's good!
The Lord sent me here,
sent me here to this spot.
He told me to tell you,
He loves you a lot!"

The people all cheered,
for God's love they now knew.
Jonah thought to himself
that he'd learned something too ...

It's never too clever
to run from God's wish.
Or you just might end up
being food for a fish.